BIG BLONDE

AND OTHER STORIES

DOROTHY PARKER

BIG BLONDE

AND OTHER STORIES

penguin books

PENGUIN BOOKS

Published by the Penguin Group

Penguin Books USA Inc., 375 Hudson Street,
New York, New York 10014, U.S.A.
Penguin Books Ltd, 27 Wrights Lane,
London W8 5TZ, England
Penguin Books Australia Ltd, Ringwood,
Victoria, Australia
Penguin Books Canada Ltd, 10 Alcorn Avenue,
Toronto, Ontario, Canada M4V 3B2
Penguin Books (N.Z.) Ltd, 182–190 Wairau Road,
Auckland 10, New Zealand

Penguin Books Ltd, Registered Offices:
Harmondsworth, Middlesex, England

Published in Penguin Books 1995

These three stories appear in *The Portable Dorothy Parker*
published by Penguin Books.

ISBN 0 14 60.0076 5

Printed in the United States of America

CONTENTS

Big Blonde 1

The Sexes 32

Dusk Before Fireworks 38

Big Blonde

Hazel Morse was a large, fair woman of the type that incites some men when they use the word "blonde" to click their tongues and wag their heads roguishly. She prided herself upon her small feet and suffered for her vanity, boxing them in snub-toed, high-heeled slippers of the shortest bearable size. The curious things about her were her hands, strange terminations to the flabby white arms splattered with pale tan spots— long, quivering hands with deep and convex nails. She should not have disfigured them with little jewels.

She was not a woman given to recollections. At her middle thirties, her old days were a blurred and flickering sequence, an imperfect film, dealing with the actions of strangers.

In her twenties, after the deferred death of a hazy widowed mother, she had been employed as a model in a wholesale dress establishment—it was still the day of the big woman, and she was then prettily colored and erect and high-breasted. Her job was not onerous, and she met numbers of men and spent numbers of evenings with them, laughing at their jokes and telling them she loved their neckties. Men liked her, and she took it for granted that the liking of many men was a desirable thing. Popularity seemed to her to be worth all the work that had to be put into its achievement. Men liked you because you were fun, and when they liked you they took you out, and there you were. So, and successfully, she was fun. She was a good sport. Men like a good sport.

No other form of diversion, simpler or more complicated, drew her attention. She never pondered if she might not be better occupied doing something else. Her ideas, or, better, her acceptances, ran right along with those of the other substantially built blondes in whom she found her friends.

When she had been working in the dress establishment some years she met Herbie Morse. He was thin, quick, attractive, with shifting lines about his shiny, brown eyes and a habit of fiercely biting at the skin around his finger nails. He drank largely; she found that entertaining. Her habitual greeting to him was an allusion to his state of the previous night.

"Oh, what a peach you had," she used to say, through her easy laugh. "I thought I'd die, the way you kept asking the waiter to dance with you."

She liked him immediately upon their meeting. She was enormously amused at his fast, slurred sentences, his interpolations of apt phrases from vaudeville acts and comic strips; she thrilled at the feel of his lean arm tucked firm beneath the sleeve of her coat; she wanted to touch the wet, flat surface of his hair. He was as promptly drawn to her. They were married six weeks after they had met.

She was delighted at the idea of being a bride; coquetted with it, played upon it. Other offers of marriage she had had, and not a few of them, but it happened that they were all from stout, serious men who had visited the dress establishment as buyers; men from Des Moines and Houston and Chicago and, in her phrase, even funnier places. There was always something immensely comic to her in the thought of living else-where than New York. She could not regard as serious proposals that she share a western residence.

She wanted to be married. She was nearing thirty now, and she did not take the years well. She spread and softened, and her darkening hair turned her to inexpert dabblings with peroxide. There were times when she had little flashes of fear about her job. And she had had a couple of thousand evenings of being a good sport among her male acquaintances. She had come to be more conscientious than spontaneous about it.

Herbie earned enough, and they took a little apartment far uptown. There was a Mission-furnished dining-room with a hanging central light globed in liver-colored glass; in the living-room were an "over-stuffed suite," a Boston fern, and a reproduction of the Henner "Magdalene" with the red hair and the blue draperies; the bedroom was in gray enamel and old rose, with Herbie's photograph on Hazel's dressing-table and Hazel's likeness on Herbie's chest of drawers.

She cooked—and she was a good cook—and marketed and chatted with the delivery boys and the colored laundress. She loved the flat, she loved her life, she loved Herbie. In the first months of their marriage, she gave him all the passion she was ever to know.

She had not realized how tired she was. It was a delight, a new game, a holiday, to give up being a good sport. If her head ached or her arches throbbed, she complained piteously, babyishly. If her mood was quiet, she did not talk. If tears came to her eyes, she let them fall.

She fell readily into the habit of tears during the first year of her marriage. Even in her good sport days, she had been known to weep lavishly and disinterestedly on occasion. Her behavior at the theater was a standing joke. She could weep at anything in a play—tiny garments, love both unrequited and mutual, seduction, purity, faithful servitors, wedlock, the triangle.

"There goes Haze," her friends would say, watching her. "She's off again."

Wedded and relaxed, she poured her tears freely. To her who had laughed so much, crying was delicious. All sorrows became her sorrows; she was Tenderness. She would cry long and softly over newspaper accounts of kidnaped babies, deserted wives, unemployed men, strayed cats, heroic dogs. Even when the paper was no longer before her, her mind revolved upon these things and the drops slipped rhythmically over her plump cheeks.

"Honestly," she would say to Herbie, "all the sadness there is in the world when you stop to think about it!"

"Yeah," Herbie would say.

She missed nobody. The old crowd, the people who had brought her and Herbie together, dropped from their lives, lingeringly at first. When she thought of this at all, it was only to consider it fitting. This was marriage. This was peace.

But the thing was that Herbie was not amused.

For a time, he had enjoyed being alone with her. He found the voluntary isolation novel and sweet. Then it palled with a ferocious suddenness. It was as if one night, sitting with her in the steam-heated living-room, he would ask no more; and the next night he was through and done with the whole thing.

He became annoyed by her misty melancholies. At first, when he came home to find her softly tired and moody, he kissed her

4

neck and patted her shoulder and begged her to tell her Herbie what was wrong. She loved that. But time slid by, and he found that there was never anything really, personally, the matter.

"Ah, for God's sake," he would say. "Crabbing again. All right, sit here and crab your head off. I'm going out."

And he would slam out of the flat and come back late and drunk.

She was completely bewildered by what happened to their marriage. First they were lovers; and then, it seemed without transition, they were enemies. She never understood it.

There were longer and longer intervals between his leaving his office and his arrival at the apartment. She went through agonies of picturing him run over and bleeding, dead and covered with a sheet. Then she lost her fears for his safety and grew sullen and wounded. When a person wanted to be with a person, he came as soon as possible. She desperately wanted him to want to be with her; her own hours only marked the time till he would come. It was often nearly nine o'clock before he came home to dinner. Always he had had many drinks, and their effect would die in him, leaving him loud and querulous and bristling for affronts.

He was too nervous, he said, to sit and do nothing for an evening. He boasted, probably not in all truth, that he had never read a book in his life.

"What am I expected to do—sit around this dump on my tail all night?" he would ask, rhetorically. And again he would slam out.

She did not know what to do. She could not manage him. She could not meet him.

She fought him furiously. A terrific domesticity had come upon her, and she would bite and scratch to guard it. She wanted what she called "a nice home." She wanted a sober, tender husband, prompt at dinner, punctual at work. She wanted sweet, comforting evenings. The idea of intimacy with other men was terrible to her; the thought that Herbie might be seeking entertainment in other women set her frantic.

It seemed to her that almost everything she read—novels from the drug-store lending library, magazine stories, women's pages in the papers—dealt with wives who lost their husbands' love. She could bear those, at that, better than accounts of neat, companionable marriage and living happily ever after.

She was frightened. Several times when Herbie came home in the evening, he found her determinedly dressed—she had had to alter those of her clothes that were not new, to make them fasten—and rouged.

"Let's go wild tonight, what do you say?" she would hail him. "A person's got lots of time to hang around and do nothing when they're dead."

So they would go out, to chop houses and the less expensive cabarets. But it turned out badly. She could no longer find amusement in watching Herbie drink. She could not laugh at his whimsicalities, she was so tensely counting his indulgences. And she was unable to keep back her remonstrances—"Ah, come on, Herb, you've had enough, haven't you? You'll feel something terrible in the morning."

He would be immediately enraged. All right, crab; crab, crab, crab, crab, that was all she ever did. What a lousy sport *she* was! There would be scenes, and one or the other of them would rise and stalk out in fury.

She could not recall the definite day that she started drinking, herself. There was nothing separate about her days. Like drops upon a window-pane, they ran together and trickled away. She had been married six months; then a year; then three years.

She had never needed to drink, formerly. She could sit for most of a night at a table where the others were imbibing earnestly and never droop in looks or spirits, nor be bored by the doings of those about her. If she took a cocktail, it was so unusual as to cause twenty minutes or so of jocular comment. But now anguish was in her. Frequently, after a quarrel, Herbie would stay out for the night, and she could not learn from him where the time had been spent. Her heart felt tight and sore in her breast, and her mind turned like an electric fan.

She hated the taste of liquor. Gin, plain or in mixtures, made her promptly sick. After experiment, she found that Scotch whisky was the best for her. She took it without water, because that was the quickest way to its effect.

Herbie pressed it on her. He was glad to see her drink. They both felt it might restore her high spirits, and their good times together might again be possible.

" 'Atta girl," he would approve her. "Let's see you get boiled, baby."

But it brought them no nearer. When she drank with him, there would be a little while of gaiety and then, strangely without beginning, they would be in a wild quarrel. They would wake in the morning not sure what it had all been about, foggy as to what had been said and done, but each deeply injured and bitterly resentful. There would be days of vengeful silence.

There had been a time when they had made up their quarrels, usually in bed. There would be kisses and little names and assurances of fresh start. . . . "Oh, it's going to be great now, Herb. We'll have swell times. I was a crab. I guess I must have been tired. But everything's going to be swell. You'll see."

Now there were no gentle reconciliations. They resumed friendly relations only in the brief magnanimity caused by liquor, before more liquor drew them into new battles. The scenes became more violent. There were shouted invectives and pushes, and sometimes sharp slaps. Once she had a black eye. Herbie was horrified next day at sight of it. He did not go to work; he followed her about, suggesting remedies and heaping dark blame on himself. But after they had had a few drinks—"to pull themselves together"—she made so many wistful references to her bruise that he shouted at her and rushed out and was gone for two days.

Each time he left the place in a rage, he threatened never to come back. She did not believe him, nor did she consider separation. Somewhere in her head or her heart was the lazy, nebulous hope that things would change and she and Herbie settle suddenly into soothing married life. Here were her home, her furniture, her husband, her station. She summoned no alternatives.

She could no longer bustle or potter. She had no more vicarious tears; the hot drops she shed were for herself. She walked ceaselessly about the rooms, her thoughts running mechanically round and round Herbie. In those days began the

8

hatred of being alone that she was never to overcome. You could be by yourself when things were all right, but when you were blue you got the howling horrors.

She commenced drinking alone, little, short drinks all through the day. It was only with Herbie that alcohol made her nervous and quick in offense. Alone, it blurred sharp things for her. She lived in a haze of it. Her life took on a dream-like quality. Nothing was astonishing.

A Mrs. Martin moved into the flat across the hall. She was a great blonde woman of forty, a promise in looks of what Mrs. Morse was to be. They made acquaintance, quickly became inseparable. Mrs. Morse spent her days in the opposite apartment. They drank together, to brace themselves after the drinks of the nights before.

She never confided her troubles about Herbie to Mrs. Martin. The subject was too bewildering to her to find comfort in talk. She let it be assumed that her husband's business kept him much away. It was not regarded as important; husbands, as such, played but shadowy parts in Mrs. Martin's circle.

Mrs. Martin had no visible spouse; you were left to decide for yourself whether he was or was not dead. She had an admirer, Joe, who came to see her almost nightly. Often he brought several friends with him—"The Boys," they were called. The Boys were big, red, good-humored men, perhaps forty-five, perhaps fifty. Mrs. Morse was glad of invitations to join the parties—Herbie was scarcely ever at home at night now. If he did come home, she did not visit Mrs. Martin. An evening alone with Herbie meant inevitably a quarrel, yet she would stay with him. There was always her thin and wordless idea that, maybe, this night, things would begin to be all right.

The Boys brought plenty of liquor along with them whenever they came to Mrs. Martin's. Drinking with them, Mrs. Morse became lively and good-natured and audacious. She was quickly popular. When she had drunk enough to cloud her most recent battle with Herbie, she was excited by their approbation. Crab, was she? Rotten sport, was she? Well, there were some that thought different.

Ed was one of The Boys. He lived in Utica—had "his own business" there, was the awed report—but he came to New York almost every week. He was married. He showed Mrs. Morse the then current photographs of Junior and Sister, and she praised them abundantly and sincerely. Soon it was accepted by the others that Ed was her particular friend.

He staked her when they all played poker; sat next her and occasionally rubbed his knee against hers during the game. She was rather lucky. Frequently she went home with a twenty-dollar bill or a ten-dollar bill or a handful of crumpled dollars. She was glad of them. Herbie was getting, in her words, something awful about money. To ask him for it brought an instant row.

"What the hell do you do with it?" he would say. "Shoot it all on Scotch?"

"I try to run this house half-way decent," she would retort. "Never thought of that, did you? Oh, no, his lordship couldn't be bothered with that."

Again, she could not find a definite day, to fix the beginning of Ed's proprietorship. It became his custom to kiss her on the mouth when he came in, as well as for farewell, and he gave her little quick kisses of approval all through the evening. She liked this rather more than she disliked it. She never thought of his kisses when she was not with him.

He would run his hand lingeringly over her back and shoulders.

"Some dizzy blonde, eh?" he would say. "Some doll."

One afternoon she came home from Mrs. Martin's to find Herbie in the bedroom. He had been away for several nights, evidently on a prolonged drinking bout. His face was gray, his hands jerked as if they were on wires. On the bed were two old suitcases, packed high. Only her photograph remained on his bureau, and the wide doors of his closet disclosed nothing but coat-hangers.

"I'm blowing," he said. "I'm through with the whole works. I got a job in Detroit."

She sat down on the edge of the bed. She had drunk much the night before, and the four Scotches she had had with Mrs. Martin had only increased her fogginess.

"Good job?" she said.

"Oh, yeah," he said. "Looks all right."

He closed a suitcase with difficulty, swearing at it in whispers.

"There's some dough in the bank," he said. "The bank book's in your top drawer. You can have the furniture and stuff."

He looked at her, and his forehead twitched.

"God damn it, I'm through, I'm telling you," he cried. "I'm through."

"All right, all right," she said. "I heard you, didn't I?"

She saw him as if he were at one end of a cannon and she at the other. Her head was beginning to ache bumpingly, and her voice had a dreary, tiresome tone. She could not have raised it.

"Like a drink before you go?" she asked.

Again he looked at her, and a corner of his mouth jerked up.

"Cockeyed again for a change, aren't you?" he said. "That's nice. Sure, get a couple of shots, will you?"

She went to the pantry, mixed him a stiff highball, poured herself a couple of inches of whisky and drank it. Then she gave herself another portion and brought the glasses into the bedroom. He had strapped both suitcases and had put on his hat and overcoat.

He took his highball.

"Well," he said, and he gave a sudden, uncertain laugh. "Here's mud in your eye."

"Mud in your eye," she said.

They drank. He put down his glass and took up the heavy suitcases.

"Got to get a train around six," he said.

She followed him down the hall. There was a song, a song that Mrs. Martin played doggedly on the phonograph, running loudly through her mind. She had never liked the thing.

> "Night and daytime,
> Always playtime.
> Ain't we got fun?"

At the door he put down the bags and faced her.

"Well," he said. "Well, take care of yourself. You'll be all right, will you?"

"Oh, sure," she said.

He opened the door, then came back to her, holding out his hand.

" 'By, Haze," he said. "Good luck to you."

She took his hand and shook it.

"Pardon my wet glove," she said.

When the door had closed behind him, she went back to the pantry.

She was flushed and lively when she went in to Mrs. Martin's that evening. The Boys were there, Ed among them. He was glad to be in town, frisky and loud and full of jokes. But she spoke quietly to him for a minute.

"Herbie blew today," she said. "Going to live out west."

"That so?" he said. He looked at her and played with the fountain pen clipped to his waistcoat pocket.

"Think he's gone for good, do you?" he asked.

"Yeah," she said. "I know he is. I know. Yeah."

"You going to live on across the hall just the same?" he said. "Know what you're going to do?"

"Gee, I don't know," she said. "I don't give much of a damn."

"Oh, come on, that's no way to talk," he told her. "What you need—you need a little snifter. How about it?"

"Yeah," she said. "Just straight."

She won forty-three dollars at poker. When the game broke up, Ed took her back to her apartment.

"Got a little kiss for me?" he asked.

He wrapped her in his big arms and kissed her violently. She was entirely passive. He held her away and looked at her.

"Little tight, honey?" he asked, anxiously. "Not going to be sick, are you?"

"Me?" she said. "I'm swell."

II

When Ed left in the morning, he took her photograph with him. He said he wanted her picture to look at, up in Utica. "You can have that one on the bureau," she said.

She put Herbie's picture in a drawer, out of her sight. When she could look at it, she meant to tear it up. She was fairly successful in keeping her mind from racing around him. Whisky slowed it for her. She was almost peaceful, in her mist.

She accepted her relationship with Ed without question or enthusiasm. When he was away, she seldom thought definitely of him. He was good to her; he gave her frequent presents and a regular allowance. She was even able to save. She did not plan ahead of any day, but her wants were few, and you might as well put money in the bank as have it lying around.

When the lease of her apartment neared its end, it was Ed who suggested moving. His friendship with Mrs. Martin and Joe had become strained over a dispute at poker; a feud was impending.

"Let's get the hell out of here," Ed said. "What I want you to have is a place near the Grand Central. Make it easier for me."

So she took a little flat in the Forties. A colored maid came in every day to clean and to make coffee for her—she was "through with that housekeeping stuff," she said, and Ed, twenty years married to a passionately domestic woman, admired this romantic uselessness and felt doubly a man of the world in abetting it.

The coffee was all she had until she went out to dinner, but alcohol kept her fat. Prohibition she regarded only as a basis for jokes. You could always get all you wanted. She was never noticeably drunk and seldom nearly sober. It required a larger daily allowance to keep her misty-minded. Too little, and she was achingly melancholy.

Ed brought her to Jimmy's. He was proud, with the pride of the transient who would be mistaken for a native, in his knowledge of small, recent restaurants occupying the lower floors of shabby brownstone houses; places where, upon mentioning the name of an habitué friend, might be obtained strange whisky and fresh gin in many of their ramifications. Jimmy's place was the favorite of his acquaintances.

There, through Ed, Mrs. Morse met many men and women, formed quick friendships. The men often took her out when Ed was in Utica. He was proud of her popularity.

She fell into the habit of going to Jimmy's alone when she had no engagement. She was certain to meet some people she knew, and join them. It was a club for her friends, both men and women.

The women at Jimmy's looked remarkably alike, and this was curious, for, through feuds, removals, and opportunities of more profitable contacts, the personnel of the group changed constantly. Yet always the newcomers resembled those whom they replaced. They were all big women and stout, broad of shoulder and abundantly breasted, with faces thickly clothed in soft, high-colored flesh. They laughed loud and often, showing opáque and lusterless teeth like squares of crockery. There was about them the health of the big, yet a slight, unwholesome suggestion of stubborn preservation. They might have been thirty-six or forty-five or anywhere between.

They composed their titles of their own first names with their husbands' surnames—Mrs. Florence Miller, Mrs. Vera Riley, Mrs. Lilian Block. This gave at the same time the solidity of marriage and the glamour of freedom. Yet only one or two were actually divorced. Most of them never referred to their dimmed spouses; some, a shorter time separated, described them in terms of great biological interest. Several were mothers, each of an only child—a boy at school somewhere, or a girl being cared for by a grandmother. Often, well on towards morning, there would be displays of kodak portraits and of tears.

They were comfortable women, cordial and friendly and irrepressibly matronly. Theirs was the quality of ease. Become fatalistic, especially about money matters, they were unworried. Whenever their funds dropped alarmingly, a new donor appeared; this had always happened. The aim of each was to have one man, permanently, to pay all her bills, in return for which she would have immediately given up other admirers and probably would have become exceedingly fond of him; for the affections of all of them were, by now, unexacting, tranquil, and easily arranged. This end, however, grew increasingly difficult yearly. Mrs. Morse was regarded as fortunate.

Ed had a good year, increased her allowance and gave her a sealskin coat. But she had to be careful of her moods with him. He insisted upon gaiety. He would not listen to admissions of aches or weariness.

16

"Hey, listen," he would say, "I got worries of my own, and plenty. Nobody wants to hear other people's troubles, sweetie. What you got to do, you got to be a sport and forget it. See? Well, slip us a little smile, then. That's my girl."

She never had enough interest to quarrel with him as she had with Herbie, but she wanted the privilege of occasional admitted sadness. It was strange. The other women she saw did not have to fight their moods. There was Mrs. Florence Miller who got regular crying jags, and the men sought only to cheer and comfort her. The others spent whole evenings in grieved recitals of worries and ills; their escorts paid them deep sympathy. But she was instantly undesirable when she was low in spirits. Once, at Jimmy's, when she could not make herself lively, Ed had walked out and left her.

"Why the hell don't you stay home and not go spoiling everybody's evening?" he had roared.

Even her slightest acquaintances seemed irritated if she were not conspicuously light-hearted.

"What's the matter with you, anyway?" they would say. "Be your age, why don't you? Have a little drink and snap out of it."

When her relationship with Ed had continued nearly three years, he moved to Florida to live. He hated leaving her; he gave her a large check and some shares of a sound stock, and his pale eyes were wet when he said good-by. She did not miss him. He came to New York infrequently, perhaps two or three times a year, and hurried directly from the train to see her. She was always pleased to have him come and never sorry to see him go.

Charley, an acquaintance of Ed's that she had met at Jimmy's, had long admired her. He had always made opportunities of touching her and leaning close to talk to her. He asked repeatedly of all their friends if they had ever heard such a fine laugh as she had. After Ed left, Charley became the main figure in her life. She classified him and spoke of him as "not so bad." There was nearly a year of Charley; then she divided her time between him and Sydney, another frequenter of Jimmy's; then Charley slipped away altogether.

Sydney was a little, brightly dressed, clever Jew. She was perhaps nearest contentment with him. He amused her always; her laughter was not forced.

He admired her completely. Her softness and size delighted him. And he thought she was great, he often told her, because she kept gay and lively when she was drunk.

"Once I had a gal," he said, "used to try and throw herself out of the window every time she got a can on. Jee-*zuss,*" he added, feelingly.

Then Sydney married a rich and watchful bride, and then there was Billy. No—after Sydney came Ferd, then Billy. In her haze, she never recalled how men entered her life and left it. There were no surprises. She had no thrill at their advent, nor woe at their departure. She seemed to be always able to attract men. There was never another as rich as Ed, but they were all generous to her, in their means.

Once she had news of Herbie. She met Mrs. Martin dining at Jimmy's, and the old friendship was vigorously renewed. The still admiring Joe, while on a business trip, had seen Herbie. He had settled in Chicago, he looked fine, he was living with some woman—seemed to be crazy about her. Mrs. Morse had been drinking vastly that day. She took the news with mild interest, as one hearing of the sex peccadilloes of somebody whose name is, after a moment's groping, familiar.

"Must be damn near seven years since I saw him," she commented. "Gee. Seven years."

More and more, her days lost their individuality. She never knew dates, nor was sure of the day of the week.

"My God, was that a year ago!" she would exclaim, when an event was recalled in conversation.

She was tired so much of the time. Tired and blue. Almost everything could give her the blues. Those old horses she saw on Sixth Avenue—struggling and slipping along the car-tracks, or standing at the curb, their heads dropped level with their worn knees. The tightly stored tears would squeeze from her eyes as she teetered past on her aching feet in the stubby, champagne-colored slippers.

The thought of death came and stayed with her and lent her a sort of drowsy cheer. It would be nice, nice and restful, to be dead.

There was no settled, shocked moment when she first thought of killing herself; it seemed to her as if the idea had always been with her. She pounced upon all the accounts of suicides in the newspapers. There was an epidemic of self-killings—or maybe it was just that she searched for the stories of them so eagerly that she found many. To read of them roused reassurance in her; she felt a cozy solidarity with the big company of the voluntary dead.

She slept, aided by whisky, till deep into the afternoons,

then lay abed, a bottle and glass at her hand, until it was time to dress to go out for dinner. She was beginning to feel towards alcohol a little puzzled distrust, as toward an old friend who has refused a simple favor. Whisky could still soothe her for most of the time, but there were sudden, inexplicable moments when the cloud fell treacherously away from her, and she was sawed by the sorrow and bewilderment and nuisance of all living. She played voluptuously with the thought of cool, sleepy retreat. She had never been troubled by religious belief and no vision of an after-life intimidated her. She dreamed by day of never again putting on tight shoes, of never having to laugh and listen and admire, of never more being a good sport. Never.

But how would you do it? It made her sick to think of jumping from heights. She could not stand a gun. At the theater, if one of the actors drew a revolver, she crammed her fingers into her ears and could not even look at the stage until after the shot had been fired. There was no gas in her flat. She looked long at the bright blue veins in her slim wrists—a cut with a razor blade, and there you'd be. But it would hurt, hurt like hell, and there would be blood to see. Poison—something tasteless and quick and painless—was the thing. But they wouldn't sell it to you in drugstores, because of the law.

She had few other thoughts.

There was a new man now—Art. He was short and fat and exacting and hard on her patience when he was drunk. But there had been only occasionals for some time before him, and she was glad of a little stability. Too, Art must be away for weeks at a stretch, selling silks, and that was restful. She was convincingly gay with him, though the effort shook her.

"The best sport in the world," he would murmur, deep in her neck. "The best sport in the world."

One night, when he had taken her to Jimmy's, she went into the dressing-room with Mrs. Florence Miller. There, while designing curly mouths on their faces with lip-rouge, they compared experiences of insomnia.

"Honestly," Mrs. Morse said, "I wouldn't close an eye if I didn't go to bed full of Scotch. I lie there and toss and turn and toss and turn. Blue! Does a person get blue lying awake that way!"

"Say, listen Hazel," Mrs. Miller said, impressively, "I'm telling you I'd be awake for a year if I didn't take veronal. That stuff makes you sleep like a fool."

"Isn't it poison, or something?" Mrs. Morse asked.

"Oh, you take too much and you're out for the count," said Mrs. Miller. "I just take five grains—they come in tablets. I'd be scared to fool around with it. But five grains, and you cork off pretty."

"Can you get it anywhere?" Mrs. Morse felt superbly Machiavellian.

"Get all you want in Jersey," said Mrs. Miller. "They won't give it to you here without you have a doctor's prescription. Finished? We'd better go back and see what the boys are doing."

That night, Art left Mrs. Morse at the door of her apartment; his mother was in town. Mrs. Morse was still sober, and it happened that there was no whisky left in her cupboard. She lay in bed, looking up at the black ceiling.

She rose early, for her, and went to New Jersey. She had never taken the tube, and did not understand it. So she went to the Pennsylvania Station and bought a railroad ticket to Newark. She thought of nothing in particular on the trip out. She looked at the uninspired hats of the women about her and gazed through the smeared window at the flat, gritty scene.

In Newark, in the first drug-store she came to, she asked for a tin of talcum powder, a nailbrush, and a box of veronal tablets. The powder and the brush were to make the hypnotic seem also a casual need. The clerk was entirely unconcerned. "We only keep them in bottles," he said, and wrapped up for her a little glass vial containing ten white tablets, stacked one on another.

She went to another drug-store and bought a face-cloth, an orange-wood stick, and a bottle of veronal tablets. The clerk was also uninterested.

"Well, I guess I got enough to kill an ox," she thought, and went back to the station.

At home, she put the little vials in the drawer of her dressing-table and stood looking at them with a dreamy tenderness.

"There they are, God bless them," she said, and she kissed her finger-tip and touched each bottle.

The colored maid was busy in the living room.

"Hey, Nettie," Mrs. Morse called. "Be an angel, will you? Run around to Jimmy's and get me a quart of Scotch."

She hummed while she awaited the girl's return.

During the next few days, whisky ministered to her as tenderly as it had done when she first turned to its aid. Alone, she was soothed and vague, at Jimmy's she was the gayest of the groups. Art was delighted with her.

Then, one night, she had an appointment to meet Art at Jimmy's for an early dinner. He was to leave afterward on a business excursion, to be away for a week. Mrs. Morse had been drinking all the afternoon; while she dressed to go out, she felt herself rising pleasurably from drowsiness to high spirits. But as she came out into the street the effects of the whisky deserted her completely, and she was filled with a slow, grinding wretchedness so horrible that she stood swaying on the pavement, unable for a moment to move forward. It was a gray night with spurts of mean, thin snow, and the streets shone with dark ice. As she slowly crossed Sixth Avenue, consciously dragging one foot past the other, a big, scarred horse pulling a rickety express-wagon crashed to his knees before her. The driver swore and screamed and lashed the beast insanely, bringing the whip back over his shoulder for every blow, while the horse struggled to get a footing on the slippery asphalt. A group gathered and watched with interest.

Art was waiting, when Mrs. Morse reached Jimmy's.

"What's the matter with you, for God's sake?" was his greeting to her.

"I saw a horse," she said. "Gee, I—a person feels sorry for horses. I—it isn't just horses. Everything's kind of terrible, isn't it? I can't help getting sunk."

"Ah, sunk, me eye," he said. "What's the idea of all the bellyaching? What have you got to be sunk about?"

23

"I can't help it," she said.

"Ah, help it, me eye," he said. "Pull yourself together, will you? Come on and sit down, and take that face off you."

She drank industriously and she tried hard, but she could not overcome her melancholy. Others joined them and commented on her gloom, and she could do no more for them than smile weakly. She made little dabs at her eyes with her handkerchief, trying to time her movements so they would be unnoticed, but several times Art caught her and scowled and shifted impatiently in his chair.

When it was time for him to go to his train, she said she would leave, too, and go home.

"And not a bad idea, either," he said. "See if you can't sleep yourself out of it. I'll see you Thursday. For God's sake, try and cheer up by then, will you?"

"Yeah," she said. "I will."

In her bedroom, she undressed with a tense speed wholly unlike her usual slow uncertainty. She put on her nightgown, took off her hair-net and passed the comb quickly through her dry, vari-colored hair. Then she took the two little vials from the drawer and carried them into the bathroom. The splintering misery had gone from her, and she felt the quick excitement of one who is about to receive an anticipated gift.

She uncorked the vials, filled a glass with water and stood before the mirror, a tablet between her fingers. Suddenly she bowed graciously to her reflection, and raised the glass to it.

"Well, here's mud in your eye," she said.

The tablets were unpleasant to take, dry and powdery and sticking obstinately half-way down her throat. It took her a long time to swallow all twenty of them. She stood watching her reflection with deep, impersonal interest, studying the movements of the gulping throat. Once more she spoke aloud.

"For God's sake, try and cheer up by Thursday, will you?" she said. "Well, you know what he can do. He and the whole lot of them."

She had no idea how quickly to expect effect from the veronal. When she had taken the last tablet, she stood uncertainly, wondering, still with a courteous, vicarious interest, if death would strike her down then and there. She felt in no way strange, save for a slight stirring of sickness from the effort of swallowing the tablets, nor did her reflected face look at all different. It would not be immediate, then; it might even take an hour or so.

She stretched her arms high and gave a vast yawn.

"Guess I'll go to bed," she said. "Gee, I'm nearly dead."

That struck her as comic, and she turned out the bathroom light and went in and laid herself down in her bed, chuckling softly all the time.

"Gee, I'm nearly dead," she quoted. "That's a hot one!"

III

Nettie, the colored maid, came in late the next afternoon to clean the apartment, and found Mrs. Morse in her bed. But then, that was not unusual. Usually, though, the sounds of cleaning waked her, and she did not like to wake up. Nettie, an agreeable girl, had learned to move softly about her work.

But when she had done the living-room and stolen in to tidy

25

the little square bedroom, she could not avoid a tiny clatter as she arranged the objects on the dressing-table. Instinctively, she glanced over her shoulder at the sleeper, and without warning a sickly uneasiness crept over her. She came to the bed and stared down at the woman lying there.

Mrs. Morse lay on her back, one flabby, white arm flung up, the wrist against her forehead. Her stiff hair hung untenderly along her face. The bed covers were pushed down, exposing a deep square of soft neck and a pink nightgown, its fabric worn uneven by many launderings; her great breasts, freed from their tight confiner, sagged beneath her arm-pits. Now and then she made knotted, snoring sounds, and from the corner of her opened mouth to the blurred turn of her jaw ran a lane of crusted spittle.

"Mis' Morse," Nettie called. "Oh, Mis' Morse! It's terrible late."

Mrs. Morse made no move.

"Mis' Morse," said Nettie. "Look, Mis' Morse. How'm I goin' get this bed made?"

Panic sprang upon the girl. She shook the woman's hot shoulder.

"Ah, wake up, will yuh?" she whined. "Ah, please wake up."

Suddenly the girl turned and ran out in the hall to the elevator door, keeping her thumb firm on the black, shiny button until the elderly car and its Negro attendant stood before her. She poured a jumble of words over the boy, and led him back to the apartment. He tiptoed creakingly in to the bedside; first gingerly, then so lustily that he left marks in the soft flesh, he prodded the unconscious woman.

"Hey, there!" he cried, and listened intently, as for an echo. "Jeez. Out like a light," he commented.

At his interest in the spectacle, Nettie's panic left her. Importance was big in both of them. They talked in quick, unfinished whispers, and it was the boy's suggestion that he fetch the young doctor who lived on the ground floor. Nettie hurried along with him. They looked forward to the limelit moment of breaking their news of something untoward, something pleasurably unpleasant. Mrs. Morse had become the medium of drama. With no ill wish to her, they hoped that her state was serious, that she would not let them down by being awake and normal on their return. A little fear of this determined them to make the most, to the doctor, of her present condition. "Matter of life and death," returned to Nettie from her thin store of reading. She considered startling the doctor with the phrase.

The doctor was in and none too pleased at interruption. He wore a yellow and blue striped dressing-gown, and he was lying on his sofa, laughing with a dark girl, her face scaly with inexpensive powder, who perched on the arm. Half-emptied highball glasses stood beside them, and her coat and hat were neatly hung up with the comfortable implication of a long stay.

Always something, the doctor grumbled. Couldn't let anybody alone after a hard day. But he put some bottles and instruments into a case, changed his dressing-gown for his coat and started out with the Negroes.

"Snap it up there, big boy," the girl called after him. "Don't be all night."

The doctor strode loudly into Mrs. Morse's flat and on to

the bedroom, Nettie and the boy right behind him. Mrs. Morse had not moved; her sleep was as deep, but soundless, now. The doctor looked sharply at her, then plunged his thumbs into the lidded pits above her eyeballs and threw his weight upon them. A high, sickened cry broke from Nettie.

"Look like he tryin' to push her right on th'ough the bed," said the boy. He chuckled.

Mrs. Morse gave no sign under the pressure. Abruptly the doctor abandoned it, and with one quick movement swept the covers down to the foot of the bed. With another he flung her nightgown back and lifted the thick, white legs, cross-hatched with blocks of tiny, iris-colored veins. He pinched them repeatedly, with long, cruel nips, back of the knees. She did not awaken.

"What's she been drinking?" he asked Nettie, over his shoulder.

With the certain celerity of one who knows just where to lay hands on a thing, Nettie went into the bathroom, bound for the cupboard where Mrs. Morse kept her whisky. But she stopped at the sight of the two vials, with their red and white labels, lying before the mirror. She brought them to the doctor.

"Oh, for the Lord Almighty's sweet sake!" he said. He dropped Mrs. Morse's legs, and pushed them impatiently across the bed. "What did she want to go taking that tripe for? Rotten yellow trick, that's what a thing like that is. Now we'll have to pump her out, and all that stuff. Nuisance, a thing like that is; that's what it amounts to. Here, George, take me down in the elevator. You wait here, maid. She won't do anything."

"She won't die on me, will she?" cried Nettie.

"No," said the doctor. "God, no. You couldn't kill her with an ax."

IV

After two days, Mrs. Morse came back to consciousness, dazed at first, then with a comprehension that brought with it the slow, saturating wretchedness.

"Oh, Lord, oh, Lord," she moaned, and tears for herself and for life striped her cheeks.

Nettie came in at the sound. For two days she had done the ugly, incessant tasks in the nursing of the unconscious, for two nights she had caught broken bits of sleep on the living-room couch. She looked coldly at the big, blown woman in the bed.

"What you been tryin' to do, Mis' Morse?" she said. "What kine o' work is that, takin' all that stuff?"

"Oh, Lord," moaned Mrs. Morse, again, and she tried to cover her eyes with her arms. But the joints felt stiff and brittle, and she cried out at their ache.

"Tha's no way to ack, takin' them pills," said Nettie. "You can thank you' stars you heah at all. How you feel now?"

"Oh, I feel great," said Mrs. Morse. "Swell, I feel."

Her hot, painful tears fell as if they would never stop.

"Tha's no way to take on, cryin' like that," Nettie said. "After what you done. The doctor, he says he could have you arrested, doin' a thing like that. He was fit to be tied, here."

"Why couldn't he let me alone?" wailed Mrs. Morse. "Why the hell couldn't he have?"

29

"Tha's terr'ble, Mis' Morse, swearin' an' talkin' like that," said Nettie, "after what people done for you. Here I ain' had no sleep at all for two nights, an' had to give up goin' out to my other ladies!"

"Oh, I'm sorry, Nettie," she said. "You're a peach. I'm sorry I've given you so much trouble. I couldn't help it. I just got sunk. Didn't you ever feel like doing it? When everything looks just lousy to you?"

"I wouldn' think o' no such thing," declared Nettie. "You got to cheer up. Tha's what you got to do. Everybody's got their troubles."

"Yeah," said Mrs. Morse. "I know."

"Come a pretty picture card for you," Nettie said. "Maybe that will cheer you up."

She handed Mrs. Morse a post-card. Mrs. Morse had to cover one eye with her hand, in order to read the message; her eyes were not yet focusing correctly.

It was from Art. On the back of a view of the Detroit Athletic Club he had written: "Greeting and salutations. Hope you have lost that gloom. Cheer up and don't take any rubber nickles. See you on Thursday."

She dropped the card to the floor. Misery crushed her as if she were between great smooth stones. There passed before her a slow, slow pageant of days spent lying in her flat, of evenings at Jimmy's being a good sport, making herself laugh and coo at Art and other Arts; she saw a long parade of weary horses and shivering beggars and all beaten, driven, stumbling things. Her feet throbbed as if she had crammed them into the

30

stubby champagne-colored slippers. Her heart seemed to swell and harden.

"Nettie," she cried, "for heaven's sake pour me a drink, will you?"

The maid looked doubtful.

"Now you know, Mis' Morse," she said, "you been near daid. I don' know if the doctor he let you drink nothin' yet."

"Oh, never mind him," she said. "You get me one, and bring in the bottle. Take one yourself."

"Well," said Nettie.

She poured them each a drink, deferentially leaving hers in the bathroom to be taken in solitude, and brought Mrs. Morse's glass in to her.

Mrs. Morse looked into the liquor and shuddered back from its odor. Maybe it would help. Maybe, when you had been knocked cold for a few days, your very first drink would give you a lift. Maybe whisky would be her friend again. She prayed without addressing a God, without knowing a God. Oh, please, please, let her be able to get drunk, please keep her always drunk.

She lifted the glass.

"Thanks, Nettie," she said. "Here's mud in your eye."

The maid giggled. "Tha's the way, Mis' Morse," she said. "You cheer up, now."

"Yeah," said Mrs. Morse. "Sure."

The Sexes

The young man with the scenic cravat glanced nervously down the sofa at the girl in the fringed dress. She was examining her handkerchief; it might have been the first one of its kind she had seen, so deep was her interest in its material, form, and possibilities. The young man cleared his throat, without necessity or success, producing a small, syncopated noise.

"Want a cigarette?" he said.

"No, thank you," she said. "Thank you ever so much just the same."

"Sorry I've only got these kind," he said. "You got any of your own?"

"I really don't know," she said. "I probably have, thank you."

"Because if you haven't," he said, "it wouldn't take me a minute to go up to the corner and get you some."

"Oh, thank you, but I wouldn't have you go to all that trouble for anything," she said. "It's awfully sweet of you to think of it. Thank you ever so much."

"Will you for God's sake stop thanking me?" he said.

"Really," she said, "I didn't know I was saying anything out of the way. I'm awfully sorry if I hurt your feelings. I know what it feels like to get your feelings hurt. I'm sure I didn't realize it was an insult to say 'thank you' to a person. I'm not exactly in the habit of having people swear at me because I say 'thank you' to them."

"I did not swear at you!" he said.

"Oh, you didn't?" she said. "I see."

"My God," he said, "all I said, I simply asked you if I couldn't go out and get you some cigarettes. Is there anything in that to get up in the air about?"

"Who's up in the air?" she said. "I'm sure I didn't know it was a criminal offense to say I wouldn't dream of giving you all that trouble. I'm afraid I must be awfully stupid, or something."

"Do you want me to go out and get you some cigarettes; or don't you?" he said.

"Goodness," she said, "if you want to go so much, please don't feel you have to stay here. I wouldn't have you feel you had to stay for anything."

"Ah, don't be that way, will you?" he said.

"Be what way?" she said. "I'm not being any way."

"What's the matter?" he said.

"Why, nothing," she said. "Why?"

"You've been funny all evening," he said. "Hardly said a word to me, ever since I came in."

"I'm terribly sorry you haven't been having a good time," she said. "For goodness' sakes, don't feel you have to stay here and be bored. I'm sure there are millions of places you could be having a lot more fun. The only thing, I'm a little bit sorry I didn't know before, that's all. When you said you were coming over tonight, I broke a lot of dates to go to the theater and everything. But it doesn't make a bit of difference. I'd much rather have you go and have a good time. It isn't very pleasant to sit here and feel you're boring a person to death."

"I'm not bored!" he said. "I don't want to go any place! Ah, honey, won't you tell me what's the matter? Ah, please."

"I haven't the faintest idea what you're talking about," she said. "There isn't a thing on earth the matter. I don't know what you mean."

"Yes, you do," he said. "There's something the trouble. Is it anything I've done, or anything?"

"Goodness," she said. "I'm sure it isn't any of my business, anything you do. I certainly wouldn't feel I had any right to criticize."

"Will you stop talking like that?" he said. "Will you, please?"

"Talking like what?" she said.

"You know," he said. "That's the way you were talking over the telephone today, too. You were so snotty when I called you up, I was afraid to talk to you."

"I beg your pardon," she said. "What did you say I was?"

"Well, I'm sorry," he said. "I didn't mean to say that. You get me so balled up."

"You see," she said, "I'm really not in the habit of hearing language like that. I've never had a thing like that said to me in my life."

"I told you I was sorry, didn't I?" he said. "Honest, honey, I didn't mean it. I don't know how I came to say a thing like that. Will you excuse me? Please?"

"Oh, certainly," she said. "Goodness, don't feel you have to apologize to me. It doesn't make any difference at all. It just seems a little bit funny to have somebody you were in the habit of thinking was a gentlemen come to your home and use language like that to you, that's all. But it doesn't make the slightest bit of difference."

"I guess nothing I say makes any difference to you," he said. "You seem to be sore at me."

"I'm sore at you?" she said. "I can't understand what put that idea in your head. Why should I be sore at you?"

"That's what I'm asking you," he said. "Won't you tell me what I've done? Have I done something to hurt your feelings, honey? The way you were, over the phone, you had me worried all day. I couldn't do a lick of work."

"I certainly wouldn't like to feel," she said, "that I was interfering with your work. I know there are lots of girls that don't think anything of doing things like that, but I think it's terrible. It certainly isn't very nice to sit here and have someone tell you you interfere with his business."

"I didn't say that!" he said. "I didn't say it!"

"Oh, didn't you?" she said. "Well, that was the impression I got. It must be my stupidity."

"I guess maybe I better go," he said. "I can't get right. Everything I say seems to make you sorer and sorer. Would you rather I'd go?"

"Please do just exactly whatever you like," she said. "I'm sure the last thing I want to do is have you stay here when you'd rather be some place else. Why don't you go some place where you won't be bored? Why don't you go up to Florence Leaming's? I know she'd love to have you."

"I don't want to go up to Florence Leaming's!" he said.

35

"What would I want to go up to Florence Leaming's for? She gives me a pain."

"Oh, really?" she said. "She didn't seem to be giving you so much of a pain at Elsie's party last night. I notice. I notice you couldn't even talk to anybody else, that's how much of a pain she gave you."

"Yeah, and you know why I was talking to her?" he said.

"Why, I suppose you think she's attractive," she said. "I suppose some people do. It's perfectly natural. Some people think she's quite pretty."

"I don't know whether she's pretty or not," he said. "I wouldn't know her if I saw her again. Why I was talking to her was you wouldn't even give me a tumble, last night. I came up and tried to talk to you, and you just said, 'Oh, how do you do'—just like that, 'Oh, how do you do'—and you turned right away and wouldn't look at me."

"I wouldn't look at you?" she said. "Oh, that's awfully funny. Oh, that's marvelous. You don't mind if I laugh, do you?"

"Go ahead and laugh your head off," he said. "But you wouldn't."

"Well, the minute you came in the room," she said, "you started making such a fuss over Florence Leaming, I thought you never wanted to see anybody else. You two seemed to be having such a wonderful time together, goodness knows I wouldn't have butted in for anything."

"My God," he said, "this what's-her-name girl came up and began talking to me before I even saw anybody else, and what could I do? I couldn't sock her in the nose, could I?"

"I certainly didn't see you try," she said.

"You saw me try to talk to you, didn't you?" he said. "And what did you do? 'Oh, how do you do.' Then this what's-her-name came up again, and there I was, stuck. Florence Leaming! I think she's terrible. Know what I think of her? I think she's a damn little fool. That's what I think of her."

"Well, of course," she said, "that's the impression she always gave me, but I don't know. I've heard people say she's pretty. Honestly I have."

"Why, she can't be pretty in the same room with you," he said.

"She has got an awfully funny nose," she said. "I really feel sorry for a girl with a nose like that."

"She's got a terrible nose," he said. "You've got a beautiful nose. Gee, you've got a pretty nose."

"Oh, I have not," she said. "You're crazy."

"And beautiful eyes," he said, "and beautiful hair and a beautiful mouth. And beautiful hands. Let me have one of the little hands. Ah, look atta little hand! Who's got the prettiest hands in the world? Who's the sweetest girl in the world?"

"I don't know," she said. "Who?"

"You don't know!" he said. "You do so, too, know."

"I do not," she said. "Who? Florence Leaming?"

"Oh, Florence Leaming, my eye!" he said. "Getting sore about Florence Leaming! And me not sleeping all last night and not doing a stroke of work all day because you wouldn't speak to me! A girl like you getting sore about a girl like Florence Leaming!"

"I think you're just perfectly crazy," she said. "I was not sore! What on earth ever made you think I was? You're simply crazy. Ow, my new pearl beads! Wait a second till I take them off. There!"

Dusk Before Fireworks

He was a very good-looking young man indeed, shaped to be annoyed. His voice was intimate as the rustle of sheets, and he kissed easily. There was no tallying the gifts of Charvet handkerchiefs, *art moderne* ash-trays, monogrammed dressing-gowns, gold keychains, and cigarette-cases of thin wood, inlaid with views of Parisian comfort stations, that were sent him by ladies too quickly confident, and were paid for with the money of unwitting husbands, which is acceptable any place in the world. Every woman who visited his small, square apartment promptly flamed with the desire to assume charge of its redecoration. During his tenancy, three separate ladies had achieved this ambition. Each had left behind her, for her brief monument, much too much glazed chintz.

The glare of the latest upholstery was dulled, now, in an April dusk. There was a soft blur of mauve and gray over chairs and curtains, instead of the daytime pattern of heroic-sized double poppies and small, sad elephants. (The most recent of the volunteer decorators was a lady who added interest to her ways by collecting all varieties of elephants save those alive or stuffed; her selection of chintz had been made less for the cause of contemporary design than in the hope of keeping ever present the wistful souvenirs of her hobby and, hence, of herself. Unhappily, the poppies, those flowers for forgetfulness, turned out to be predominant in the pattern.)

The very good-looking young man was stretched in a chair that was legless and short in back. It was a strain to see in that chair any virtue save the speeding one of modernity. Certainly it was a peril to all who dealt with it; they were far from their best within its arms, and they could never have wished to be remembered as they appeared while easing into its depths or struggling out again. All, that is, save the young man. He was a long young man, broad at the shoulders and chest and narrow everywhere else, and his muscles obeyed him at the exact instant of command. He rose and lay, he moved and was still, always in beauty. Several men disliked him, but only one woman really hated him. She was his sister. She was stump-shaped, and she had straight hair.

On the sofa opposite the difficult chair there sat a young woman, slight and softly dressed. There was no more to her frock than some dull, dark silk and a little chiffon, but the recurrent bill for it demanded, in bitter black and white, a sum well on toward the second hundred. Once the very good-looking young man had said that he liked women in quiet and conservative clothes, carefully made. The young woman was of those unfortunates who remember every word. This made living peculiarly trying for her when it was later demonstrated that the young man was also partial to ladies given to garments of slap-dash cut, and color like the sound of big brass instruments.

The young woman was temperately pretty in the eyes of most beholders; but there were a few, mainly hand-to-mouth people, artists and such, who could not look enough at her. Half a year before, she had been sweeter to see. Now there was tension about her mouth and unease along her brow, and her eyes looked wearied and troubled. The gentle dusk became her. The young man who shared it with her could not see these things.

She stretched her arms and laced her fingers high above her head.

"Oh, this is nice," she said. "It's nice being here."

"It's nice and peaceful," he said. "Oh, Lord. Why can't people just be peaceful? That's little enough to ask, isn't it? Why does there have to be so much hell, all the time?"

She dropped her hands to her lap.

"There doesn't have to be at all," she said. She had a quiet voice, and she said her words with every courtesy to each of them, as if she respected language. "There's never any need for hell."

"There's an awful lot of it around, sweet," he said.

"There certainly is," she said. "There's just as much hell as there are hundreds of little shrill, unnecessary people. It's the second-raters that stir up hell; first-rate people wouldn't. You need never have another bit of it in your beautiful life if—you'll pardon my pointing—you could just manage to steel yourself against that band of spitting hell-cats that is included in your somewhat overcrowded acquaintance, my lamb. Ah, but I mean it, Hobie, dear. I've been wanting to tell you for so long. But it's so rotten hard to say. If I say it, it makes me sound just like one of them—makes me seem inexpensive and jealous. Surely, you know, after all this time, I'm not like that.

40

It's just that I worry so about you. You're so fine, you're so lovely, it nearly kills me to see you just eaten up by a lot of things like Margot Wadsworth and Mrs. Holt and Evie Maynard and those. You're so much better than that. You know that's why I'm saying it. You know I haven't got a stitch of jealousy in me. Jealous! Good heavens, if I were going to be jealous, I'd be it about someone worth while, and not about any silly, stupid, idle, worthless, selfish, hysterical, vulgar, promiscuous, sex-ridden—"

"Darling!" he said.

"Well, I'm sorry," she said. "I guess I'm sorry. I didn't really mean to go into the subject of certain of your friends. Maybe the way they behave isn't their fault, said she, lying in her teeth. After all, you can't expect them to know what it's about. Poor things, they'll never know how sweet it can be, how lovely it always is when we're alone together. It is, isn't it? Ah, Hobie, isn't it?"

The young man raised his slow lids and looked at her. He smiled with one end of his beautiful curly mouth.

"Uh-huh," he said.

He took his eyes from hers and became busy with an ash-tray and a spent cigarette. But he still smiled.

"Ah, don't," she said. "You promised you'd forget about—about last Wednesday. You said you'd never remember it again. Oh, whatever made me do it! Making scenes. Having tantrums. Rushing out into the night. And then coming crawling back. Me, that wanted to show you how different a woman could be! Oh, please, please don't let's think about it. Only tell me I wasn't as terrible as I know I was."

"Darling," he said, for he was often a young man of simple statements, "you were the worst I ever saw."

"And doesn't that come straight from Sir Hubert!" she said. "Oh, dear. Oh, dear, oh, dear. What can I say? 'Sorry' isn't nearly enough. I'm broken. I'm in little bits. Would you mind doing something about putting me together again?"

She held out her arms to him.

The young man rose, came over to the sofa, and kissed her. He had intended a quick, good-humored kiss, a moment's stop on a projected trip out to his little pantry to mix cocktails. But her arms clasped him so close and so gladly that he dismissed the plan. He lifted her to her feet, and did not leave her.

Presently she moved her head and hid her face above his heart.

"Listen," she said, against cloth. "I want to say it all now, and then never say it any more. I want to tell you that there'll never, never be anything like last Wednesday again. What we have is so much too lovely ever to cheapen. I promise, oh, I promise you, I won't ever be like—like anybody else."

"You couldn't be, Kit," he said.

"Ah, think that always," she said, "and say it sometimes. It's so sweet to hear. Will you, Hobie?"

"For your size," he said, "You talk an awful lot." His fingers slid to her chin and he held her face for his greater convenience.

After a while she moved again.

"Guess who I'd rather be, right this minute, than anybody in the whole world," she said.

"Who?" he said.

42

"Me," she said.

The telephone rang.

The telephone was in the young man's bedroom, standing in frequent silence on the little table by his bed. There was no door to the bed-chamber; a plan which had disadvantages, too. Only a curtained archway sequestered its intimacies from those of the living-room. Another archway, also streaming chintz, gave from the bedroom upon a tiny passage, along which were ranged the bathroom and the pantry. It was only by entering either of these, closing the door behind, and turning the faucets on to the full that any second person in the apartment could avoid hearing what was being said over the telephone. The young man sometimes thought of removing to a flat of more sympathetic design.

"There's that damn telephone," the young man said.

"Isn't it?" the young woman said. "And wouldn't it be?"

"Let's not answer it," he said. "Let's let it ring."

"No, you mustn't," she said. "I must be big and strong. Anyway, maybe it's only somebody that just died and left you twenty million dollars. Maybe it isn't some other woman at all. And if it is, what difference does it make? See how sweet and reasonable I am? Look at me being generous."

"You can afford to be, sweetheart," he said.

"I know I can," she said. "After all, whoever she is, she's way off on an end of a wire, and I'm right here."

She smiled up at him. So it was nearly half a minute before he went away to the telephone.

Still smiling, the young woman stretched her head back, closed her eyes and flung her arms wide. A long sigh raised her breast. Thus she stood, then she went and settled back on the sofa. She essayed whistling softly, but the issuing sounds would not resemble the intended tune and she felt, though interested, vaguely betrayed. Then she looked about the dusk-filled room. Then she pondered her finger nails, bringing each bent hand close to her eyes, and could find no fault. Then she smoothed her skirt along her legs and shook out the chiffon frills at her wrists. Then she spread her little handkerchief on her knee and with exquisite care traced the "Katherine" embroidered in script across one of its corners. Then she gave it all up and did nothing but listen.

"Yes?" the young man was saying. "Hello? Hello. I *told* you this is Mr. Ogden. Well, I *am* holding the wire. I've *been* holding the wire. *You're* the one that went away. Hello? Ah, now listen—Hello? Hey. Oh, what the hell *is* this? Come back, will you? Operator! Hello, *Yes,* this is Mr. Ogden. Who? Oh, hello, Connie. How are you, dear? What? You're what? Oh, that's too bad. What's the matter? Why can't you? Where are you, in Greenwich? Oh, I see. When, now? Why, Connie, the only thing is I've got to go right out. So if you came in to town now, it really wouldn't do much—Well, I couldn't very well do that, dear. I'm keeping these people waiting as it is. I say I'm late now, I was just going out the door when you called. Why, I'd better not say that, Connie, because there's no telling when I'll be able to break away. Look, why don't you wait and come in to town tomorrow some time? What? Can't you tell me now? Oh—Well—Oh, Connie, there's no reason to talk like that. Why, of course I'd do anything in the world I could, but I tell you I can't tonight. No, no, no, no, no, it isn't that at all.

No, it's nothing like that, I tell you. These people are friends of my sister's, and it's just one of those things you've got to do. Why don't you be a good girl and go to bed early, and then you'll feel better tomorrow? Hm? Will you do that? What? Of course I do, Connie. I'll try later on if I can, dear. Well, all right, if you want to, but I don't know what time I'll be home. Of course I do. Of course I do. Yes, *do*, Connie. You be a good girl, won't you? 'By, dear."

The young man returned, through the chintz. He had a rather worn look. It was, of course, becoming to him.

"God," he said, simply.

The young woman on the sofa looked at him as if through clear ice.

"And how *is* dear Mrs. Holt?" she said.

"Great," he said. "Corking. Way up at the top of her form." He dropped wearily into the low chair. "She says she has something she wants to tell me."

"It can't be her age," she said.

He smiled without joy. "She says it's too hard to say over the wire," he said.

"Then it may be her age," she said. "She's afraid it might sound like her telephone number."

"About twice a week," he said, "Connie has something she must tell you right away, that she couldn't possibly say over the telephone. Usually it turns out she's caught the butler drinking again."

"I see," she said.

"Well," he said. "Poor little Connie."

"Poor little Connie," she said. "Oh, my God. That saber-toothed tigress. Poor little Connie."

"Darling, why do we have to waste time talking about Connie Holt?" he said. "Can't we just be peaceful?"

"Not while that she-beast prowls the streets," she said. "Is she coming in to town tonight?"

"Well, she was," he said, "but then she more or less said she wouldn't."

"Oh, she will," she said. "You get right down out of that fool's paradise you're in. She'll shoot out of Greenwich like a bat out of hell, if she thinks there's a chance of seeing you. Ah, Hobie, you don't really want to see that old thing, do you? Do you? Because if you do—Well, I suppose maybe you do. Naturally, if she has something she must tell you right away, you want to see her. Look, Hobie, you know you can see me any time. It isn't a bit important, seeing me tonight. Why don't you call up Mrs. Holt and tell her to take the next train in? She'd get here quicker by train than by motor, wouldn't she? Please go ahead and do it. It's quite all right about me. Really."

"You know," he said, "I knew that was coming. I could tell it by the way you were when I came back from the telephone. Oh, Kit, what makes you want to talk like that? You know damned well the last thing I want to do is see Connie Holt. You know how I want to be with you. Why do you want to work up all this? I watched you just sit there and deliberately talk yourself into it, starting right out of nothing. Now what's the idea of that? Oh, good Lord, what's the matter with women, anyway?"

"Please don't call me 'women' " she said.

"I'm sorry, darling," he said. "I didn't mean to use bad words." He smiled at her. She felt her heart go liquid, but she did her best to be harder won.

"Doubtless," she said, and her words fell like snow when there is no wind, "I spoke ill-advisedly. If I said, as I must have, something to distress you, I can only beg you to believe that that was my misfortune, and not my intention. It seemed to me as if I were doing only a courteous thing in suggesting that you need feel no obligation about spending the evening with me, when you would naturally wish to be with Mrs. Holt. I simply felt that—Oh, the hell with it! I'm no good at this. Of course, I didn't mean it, dearest. If you had said, 'All right,' and had gone and told her to come in, I should have died. I just said it because I wanted to hear you say it was me you wanted to be with. Oh, I need to hear you say that, Hobie. It's—it's what I live on, darling."

"Kit," he said, "you ought to know, without my saying it. You know. It's this feeling you *have* to say things—that's what spoils everything."

"I suppose so," she said. "I suppose I know so. Only—the thing is, I get so mixed up, I just—I just can't go on. I've got to be reassured, dearest. I didn't need to be at first, when everything was gay and sure, but things aren't—well, they aren't the same now. There seem to be so many others that—So I need so terribly to have you tell me that it's me and not anybody else. Oh, I *had* to have you say that, a few minutes ago. Look, Hobie. How do you think it made me feel to sit here and hear you lie to Connie Holt—to hear you say you have to go out with friends of your sister's? Now why couldn't you say you had a date with me? Are you ashamed of me, Hobie? Is that it?"

"Oh, Kit," he said, "for heaven's sake! I don't know why I did it. I did it before I even thought. I did it—well, sort of instinctively, I guess, because it seemed to be the easiest thing to do. I suppose I'm just weak."

"No!" she said. "You weak? Well! And is there any other news tonight?"

"I know I am," he said. "I know it's weak to do anything in the world to avoid a scene."

"Exactly what," she said, "is Mrs. Holt to you and you to her that she may make a scene if she learns that you have an engagement with another woman?"

"Oh, God!" he said. "I told you I don't give a damn about Connie Holt. She's nothing to me. Now will you for Gods's sake let it drop?"

"Oh, she's nothing to you," she said. "I see. Naturally, that would be why you called her 'dear' every other word."

"If I did," he said, "I never knew I was saying it. Good Lord, that doesn't mean anything. It's simply a—a form of nervousness, I suppose. I say it when I can't think what to call people. Why, I call telephone operators 'dear.' "

"I'm sure you do!" she said.

They glared. It was the young man who gave first. He went and sat close to her on the sofa, and for a while there were only murmurs. Then he said, "Will you stop? Will you stop it? Will you always be just like this—just sweet and the way you're meant to be and no fighting?"

"I will," she said. "Honest, I mean to. Let's not let anything come between us again ever. Mrs. Holt, indeed! Hell with her."

"Hell with her," he said. There was another silence, during which the young man did several things that he did extraordinarily well.

Suddenly the young woman stiffened her arms and pushed him away from her.

"And how do I know," she said, "that the way you talk to me about Connie Holt isn't just the way you talk to her about me when I'm not here? How do I know that?"

"Oh, my Lord," he said. "Oh, my dear, sweet Lord. Just when everything was all right. Ah, stop it, will you, baby? Let's just be quiet. Like this. See?"

A little later he said. "Look, sweet, how about a cocktail? Mightn't that be an idea? I'll go make them. And would you like the lights lighted?"

"Oh, no," she said. "I like it better in the dusk, like this. It's sweet. Dusk is so personal, somehow. And this way you can't see those lampshades. Hobie, if you knew how much I hate your lampshades!"

"Honestly?" he said, with less injury than bewilderment in his voice. He looked at the shades as if he saw them for the first time. They were of vellum, or some substance near it, and upon each was painted a panorama of the right bank of the Seine, with the minute windows of the buildings cut out, under the direction of a superior mind, so that light might come through. "What's the matter with them, Kit?"

"Dearest, if you don't know, I can't ever explain it to you," she said. "Among other things, they're banal, inappropriate, and unbeautiful. They're exactly what Evie Maynard *would* have chosen. She thinks, just because they show views of Paris, that they're pretty darned sophisticated. She is that not uncommon type of woman that thinks any reference to la belle France is an invitation to the waltz. 'Not uncommon.' If that isn't the mildest word-picture that ever was painted of that—"

"Don't you like the way she decorated the apartment?" he said.

"Sweetheart," she said. "I think it's poisonous. You know that."

"Would you like to do it over?" he said.

"I should say not," she said. "Look, Hobie, don't you remember me? I'm the one that doesn't want to decorate your flat. Now do you place me? But if I ever *did*, the first thing I should do would be to paint these walls putty color—no, I guess first I'd tear off all this chintz and fling it to the winds, and then I'd—"

The telephone rang.

The young man threw one stricken glance at the young woman and then sat motionless. The jangles of the bell cut the dusk like little scissors.

"I think," said the young woman, exquisitely, "that your telephone is ringing. Don't let me keep you from answering it. As a matter of fact, I really must go powder my nose."

She sprang up, dashed through the bedroom, and into the bathroom. There was the sound of a closed door, the grind of a firmly turned key, and then immediately the noise of rushing waters.

When she returned, eventually, to the living-room, the

young man was pouring a pale, cold liquid into small glasses. He gave one to her, and smiled at her over it. It was his wistful smile. It was of his best.

"Hobie," she said, "is there a livery stable anywhere around here where they rent wild horses?"

"What?" he said.

"Because if there is," she said, "I wish you'd call up and ask them to send over a couple of teams. I want to show you they couldn't drag me into asking who that was on the telephone."

"Oh," he said, and tried his cocktail. "Is this dry enough, sweet? Because you like them dry, don't you? Sure it's all right? Really? Ah, wait a second darling. Let *me* light your cigarette. There. Sure you're all right?"

"I can't stand it," she said. "I just lost all my strength of purpose—maybe the maid will find it on the floor in the morning. Hobart Ogden, who was that on the telephone?"

"Oh, that?" he said. "Well, that was a certain lady who shall be nameless."

"I'm sure she should be," she said. "She doubtless has all the other qualities of a—Well. I didn't quite say it, I'm keeping my head. Ah, dearest, was that Connie Holt again?"

"No, that was the funniest thing," he said. "That was Evie Maynard. Just when we were talking about her."

"Well, well, well," she said. "Isn't it a small world? And what's on her mind, if I may so flatter her? Is *her* butler tight, too?"

"Evie hasn't got a butler," he said. He tried smiling again, but found it better to abandon the idea and concentrate on refilling the young woman's glass. "No, she's just dizzy, the same

51

as usual. She's got a cocktail party at her apartment, and they all want to go out on the town, that's all."

"Luckily," she said, "you had to go out with these friends of your sister's. You were just going out the door when she called."

"I never told her any such thing!" he said. "I said I had a date I'd been looking forward to all week."

"Oh, you didn't mention any names?" she said.

"There's no reason why I should, to Evie Maynard," he said. "It's none of her affair, any more than what she's doing and who she's doing it with is any concern of mine. She's nothing in my life. You know that. I've hardly seen her since she did the apartment. I don't care if I never see her again. I'd *rather* I never saw her again."

"I should think that might be managed, if you've really set your heart on it," she said.

"Well, I do what I can," he said. "She wanted to come in now for a cocktail, she and some of those interior decorator boys she has with her, and I told her absolutely no."

"And you think that will keep her away?" she said. "Oh, no. She'll be here. She and her feathered friends. Let's see—they ought to arrive just about the time that Mrs. Holt has thought it over and come in to town. Well. It's shaping up into a lovely evening, isn't it?"

"Great," he said. "And if I may say so, you're doing everything you can to make it harder, you little sweet." He poured more cocktails. "Oh, Kit, why are you being so nasty? Don't do it, darling. It's not like you. It's so unbecoming to you."

"I know it's horrible," she said. "It's—well, I do it in de-

52

fense, I suppose, Hobie. If I didn't say nasty things, I'd cry. I'm afraid to cry; it would take me so long to stop. I—oh, I'm so hurt, dear. I don't know what to think. All these women. All these awful women. If they were fine, if they were sweet and gentle and intelligent, I shouldn't mind. Or maybe I should. I don't know. I don't know much of anything, any more. My mind goes round and round. I thought what we had was so different. Well—it wasn't. Sometimes I think it would be better never to see you any more. But then I know I couldn't stand that. I'm too far gone now. I'd do anything to be with you! And so I'm just another of those women to you. And I used to come first, Hobie—oh, I did! I did!"

"You did!" he said. "And you do!"

"And I always will?" she said.

"And you always will," he said, "as long as you'll only be your own self. Please be sweet again, Kit. Like this, darling. Like this, child."

Again they were close, and again there was no sound.

The telephone rang.

They started as if the same arrow had pierced them. Then the young woman moved slowly back.

"You know," she said, musingly, "this is my fault. I did this. It was me. I was the one that said let's meet here, and not at my house. I said it would be quieter, and I had so much I wanted to talk to you about. I said we could be quiet and alone here. Yes, I said that."

"I give you my word," he said, "that damn thing hasn't rung in a week."

"It was lucky for me, wasn't it?" she said, "that I happened

53

to be here the last time it did. I am known as Little Miss Horseshoes. Well. Oh, please do answer it, Hobie. It drives me even crazier to have it ring like this."

"I hope to God," the young man said, "that it's a wrong number." He held her to him, hard. "Darling," he said. Then he went to the telephone.

"Hello," he said into the receiver. "Yes? Oh, hello there. How are you, dear—how are you? Oh, did you? Ah, that's too bad. Why, you see I was out with these friends on my—I was out till quite late. Oh, you did? Oh, that's too bad, dear, you waited up all that time. No, I did *not* say that, Margot, I said I'd come if I possibly could. That's exactly what I said. I did so. Well, then you misunderstood me. Well, you must have. Now, there's no need to be unreasonable about it. Listen, what I said, I said I'd come if it was possible, but I didn't think there was a chance. If you think hard, you'll remember, dear. Well, I'm terribly sorry, but I don't see what you're making so much fuss about. It was just a misunderstanding, that's all. Why don't you calm down and be a good little girl? Won't you? Why, I can't tonight, dear. Because I *can't*. Well, I have a date I've had for a long time. Yes. Oh, no, it isn't anything like that! Oh, now, please, Margot! Margot, please don't! Now don't do that! I tell you I won't be here. All right, come ahead, but I won't be in. Listen, I can't talk to you when you're like this. I'll call you tomorrow, dear. I tell you I won't be *in*, dear! Please be good. Certainly I do. Look. I have to run now. I'll call you, dear. 'By."

The young man came back to the living-room, and sent his somewhat shaken voice ahead of him.

"How about another cocktail, sweet?" he said. "Don't you think we really ought—" Through the thickening dark, he saw the young woman. She stood straight and tense. Her fur scarf was knotted about her shoulders, and she was drawing on her second glove.

"What's this about?" the young man said.

"I'm so sorry," the young woman said, "but I truly must go home."

"Oh, really?" he said. "May I ask why?"

"It's sweet of you," she said, "to be interested enough to want to know. Thank you so much. Well, it just happens, I can't stand any more of this. There is somewhere, I think, some proverb about a worm's eventually turning. It is doubtless from the Arabic. They so often are. Well, good night, Hobie, and thank you so much for those delicious cocktails. They've cheered me up wonderfully."

She held out her hand. He caught it tight in both of his.

"Ah, now listen," he said. "Please don't do this, Kit. Please, don't, darling. Please. This is just the way you were last Wednesday."

"Yes," she said. "And for exactly the same reason. Please give me back my hand. Thank you. Well, good night, Hobie, and good luck, always."

"All right," he said. "If this is what you want to do."

"Want to do!" she said. "It's nothing *I* want. I simply felt it would be rather easier for you if you could be alone, to receive your telephone calls. Surely you cannot blame me for feeling a bit *de trop*."

"My Lord, do you think I want to talk to those fools?" he

said. "What can I do? Take the telephone receiver off? Is that what you want me to do?"

"It's a good trick of yours," she said. "I gather that was what you did last Wednesday night, when I kept trying to call you after I'd gone home, when I was in holy agony there."

"I did not!" he said. "They must have been calling the wrong number. I tell you I was alone here all the time you were gone."

"So you said," she said.

"I don't lie to you, Kit," he said.

"That," she said, "is the most outrageous lie you have ever told me. Good night, Hobie."

Only from the young man's eyes and voice could his anger be judged. The beautiful scroll of his mouth never straightened. He took her hand and bowed over it.

"Good night, Kit," he said.

"Good night," she said. "Well, good night. I'm sorry it must end like this. But if you want other things—well, they're what you want. You can't have both them and me. Good night, Hobie."

"Good night, Kit," he said.

"I'm sorry," she said. "It does seem too bad. Doesn't it?"

"It's what you want," he said.

"I?" she said. "It's what *you* do."

"Oh, Kit, can't you understand?" he said. "You always used to. Don't you know how I am? I just say things and do things that don't mean anything, just for the sake of peace, just for the sake of not having a feud. That's what gets me in trouble. You don't have to do it, I know. You're luckier than I am."

56

"Luckier?" she said. "Curious word."

"Well, stronger, then," he said. "Finer. Honester. Decenter. All those. Ah, don't do this, Kit. Please. Please take those things off, and come sit down."

"Sit down?" she said. "And wait for the ladies to gather?"

"They're not coming," he said.

"How do you know?" she said. "They've come here before, haven't they? How do you know they won't come tonight?"

"I don't know!" he said. "I don't know what the hell they'll do. I don't know what the hell you'll do, any more. And I thought you were different!"

"I was different," she said, "just so long as you thought I was different."

"Ah, Kit," he said, "Kit. Darling. Come and be the way we were. Come and be sweet and peaceful. Look. Let's have a cocktail, just to each other, and then let's go out to some quiet place for dinner, where we can talk. Will you?"

"Well—" she said. "If you think—"

"I think," he said.

The telephone rang.

"Oh, my *God!*" shrieked the young woman. "Go answer it, you damned—you damned *stallion!*"

She rushed for the door, opened it, and was gone. She was, after all, different. She neither slammed the door nor left it stark open.

The young man stood, and he shook his remarkable head slowly. Slowly, too, he turned and went into the bedroom.

He spoke into the telephone receiver drearily at first, then he seemed to enjoy both hearing and speaking. He used a woman's name in address. It was not Connie; it was not Evie; it was not Margot. Glowingly he besought the unseen one to meet him; tepidly he agreed to await her coming where he was. He besought her, then, to ring his bell first three times and then twice, for admission. No, no, no, he said, this was not for any reason that might have occurred to her; it was simply that some business friend of his had said something about dropping in, and he wanted to make sure there would be no such intruders. He spoke of his hopes, indeed his assurances, of an evening of sweetness and peace. He said "good-bye," and he said "dear."

The very good-looking young man hung up the receiver, and looked long at the dial of his wrist-watch, now delicately luminous. He seemed to be calculating. So long for a young woman to reach her home, and fling herself upon her couch, so long for tears, so long for exhaustion, so long for remorse, so long for rising tenderness. Thoughtfully he lifted the receiver from its hook and set it on end upon the little table.

Then he went into the living-room, and sped the dark before the tiny beams that sifted through the little open windows in the panoramas of Paris.